Butterfly Meadow

Joy's Close Call

Come flutter by
Butterfly Meadow!

Butterfly Meadow

Joy's Close Call

by Olivia Moss
illustrated by Helen Turner

SCHOLASTIC INC.

New York Toronto London Auckland Sydney
Mexico City New Delhi Hong Kong Buenos Aires

To Isobel and Alice Joy

With special thanks to Narinder Dhami

ISBN-13: 978-0-545-10713-6
ISBN-10: 0-545-10713-X

12 11 10 9 8 7 6 5 4   11 12 13 14/0

Printed in the U.S.A.

First printing, April 2009

Contents

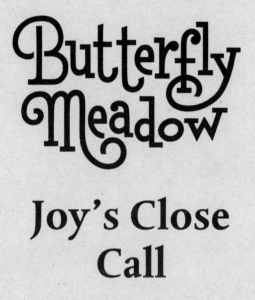

Joy's Close Call

CHAPTER ONE

A Surprise

"Hurry, Skipper!" Dazzle called. She watched the little blue butterfly swoop under the head of a daisy, then soar up to loop around the branch of an elm tree. "This could be your best time yet."

The two butterflies were having a great time flying through the obstacle

course they had made in Butterfly
Meadow! Even the occasional raindrop
wasn't enough to keep them from
playing. Skipper skimmed over a
crimson poppy and dashed toward the
finish. A friendly spider had spun them
a finish line out of a thin silvery thread
stretched between two tall clumps
of grass.

"Good job, Skipper!" Dazzle cried, flying over to her friend. "You were much faster that time."

"I'm so hot," Skipper panted, flapping her wings. "Thank goodness for the rain shower. Even though I can't touch the raindrops, they're helping to cool me down."

"I think the rain might stop soon." Dazzle glanced at the misty sky. "I can see the sun peeking through the clouds." As she watched, an arch of pale, beautiful colors appeared overhead, shimmering in the sunshine.

"Oh!" Dazzle gasped. "What's *that*, Skipper?"

Skipper turned to look. "I don't know," she breathed in awe. "I've never seen anything like it before."

"But where did it come from?" Dazzle wanted to know. Her gaze was fixed on the big, shining arch. "Look at all the different colors. I can see red, orange, and yellow —"

"And green, blue, indigo, and violet," Skipper added.

All the other butterflies in Butterfly Meadow had noticed the pretty arch, too. They were darting around, excited.

"Look! Isn't it *beautiful*?" Dazzle heard her friend Mallow cry. She turned to see the cabbage white butterfly nearby.

"Mallow," Dazzle called, "do you know what that colorful ribbon is?"

"Of course," Mallow replied, twirling happily in the air. "It's a rainbow! It appears when rain and sunshine are mixed together."

Dazzle and Skipper glanced at each other, grinning.

"Rainbow," Dazzle said softly. "What a pretty word."

"Look at me!" Twinkle swooped underneath the arch of the rainbow to join her friends. "I have almost all the same colors in my beautiful wings."

Dazzle, Skipper, and Mallow smiled as they watched their friend. Twinkle was always *very* proud of the way she looked.

"Hooray for the rainbow!" Mallow shouted, and all the butterflies cheered. "But now we have to hurry." Mallow turned to Dazzle, Skipper, and Twinkle. "Follow me!"

"Where are we going?" Dazzle wondered aloud, as the three of them fluttered after Mallow.

"I don't know," Skipper replied. "Mallow, why are we in such a hurry?"

"Beauty, the oldest and wisest butterfly in Butterfly Meadow, told me a secret," Mallow answered. The butterflies flew in closer. "She said that rainbows lead to surprises! Something special waits at the end of the rainbow."

Dazzle, Skipper, and Twinkle glanced at one another in amazement.

"The rainbow began in Butterfly Meadow, so now we have to track down the other end of it to find the surprise," Mallow said.

Dazzle couldn't wait!

CHAPTER TWO

Bluebell Wood

"Maybe it's a flower full of tasty nectar," Dazzle said.

"Or maybe it's the most beautiful butterfly in the world," Skipper suggested.

"Oh, no," Twinkle said, smiling proudly. "I'm already right here."

Dazzle couldn't help giggling.

"Tell us what the surprise is, Mallow," Skipper said eagerly.

Mallow shook her head. "Not yet," she replied. "But I'll tell you soon."

The butterflies continued flying toward the rainbow. Suddenly, Dazzle gasped.

"Look!" she called. "The colors are fading."

"Rainbows never last long," Mallow

explained. "Hurry! We need to find the end before it disappears."

The butterflies flew higher and faster. Dazzle kept glancing up anxiously at the rainbow. Soon, the beautiful colors would vanish completely.

"I can see the end of the rainbow!" Skipper shouted.

The four butterflies zoomed down the arch of the rainbow as the last ribbons of color finally disappeared.

"I know where we are," Twinkle said as they fluttered down through the trees. "I've heard all about this place. It's Bluebell Wood!"

The ground below the trees was thickly carpeted with beautiful bright blue flowers. They spread as far as the butterflies could see.

"Maybe finding this place is our surprise?" Skipper suggested as they floated above the flowers.

"Bluebell Wood *is* pretty, but it's not our surprise," Mallow replied with a smile. "Beauty told me that the rainbow is supposed to lead us to a new friend!"

Dazzle, Skipper, and Twinkle circled through the air in excitement.

"Let's see who can find our new friend first!" Dazzle said.

The four butterflies
zoomed off in different
directions. Dazzle
flew across the tops
of the bluebells,
searching behind their
pointed leaves. She
was about to fly higher and explore a
tall sycamore tree when she heard
Mallow's voice.

"Over here, everyone!"

Dazzle, Skipper, and Twinkle rushed
to join Mallow. She was hovering near
an oak tree. Her wings trembled with
excitement.

"Look!" Mallow whispered, pointing.
"Another butterfly!"

Dazzle saw a pale brown butterfly
perched on a leaf not too far away. It

had dark, round markings on its wings. They looked like eyes!

"It has eyes on its wings!" Dazzle murmured. "I've never seen *that* before."

"Hello there," Skipper called. "Excuse me, but what kind of butterfly are you?"

The butterfly spun around at the sound of Skipper's voice. It spread its wings, batting them slowly.

"Hello to you, too!" the butterfly replied cheerfully. "These marks on my

wings look like eyes, don't they? That means I'm a little wood satyr!"

Mallow gasped. "I've never met one of those before!"

The little wood satyr flew toward them, doing a wonderful bouncing dance through the air.

"Pleased to meet you," she said. "My name is Joy!"

CHAPTER THREE

Joy's Jokes

"Joy?" Dazzle repeated. "That's a pretty name."

"You must be our new friend!" Mallow said. She explained the rainbow surprise to Joy.

"Did you see the rainbow, too?" asked Twinkle.

"Oh, yes, but it's no big deal." Joy bounced around the other butterflies. "I see rainbows all the time!"

"Really?" Mallow said. "I thought they only appeared every once in a while."

"Well, I'm *very* glad this rainbow brought me some new friends!" Joy announced happily. "Hey, do you know why birds fly south for the winter?"

Dazzle thought for a moment. "I think it's because they're going somewhere warmer," she replied.

"No, silly!" Joy shook her head. "It's because it's too far to walk!"

Dazzle and
the other
butterflies giggled.

"Why don't ducks
tell jokes when they fly?"
Joy went on. "Because they'd
quack up!"

Dazzle and the others laughed so
hard that they tumbled through the air.

"I *love* telling jokes," Joy admitted,
twirling around them. "I love playing
jokes, too."

"What kind of jokes?" Dazzle
asked as Joy did a somersault. She
wondered if their new friend ever
stopped moving!

"Oh, you'll find out soon." Joy smiled.
"Are you thirsty?"

"Yes, I'd love a drink of nectar," Mallow replied. "We flew a long way to get here."

"You can drink from the bluebells," Joy said. "But I don't like nectar. Wood satyrs only drink tree sap." She flew toward a tall oak tree.

"Is this one of Joy's jokes?" Twinkle whispered, watching their new friend flutter off.

"I don't know," Dazzle replied, shrugging. Didn't *all* butterflies drink nectar? It had been a while since Dazzle had emerged from her cocoon, but she still had a lot to learn.

Dazzle, Twinkle, Skipper, and Mallow flew down and landed lightly on some of the beautiful bluebells. Dazzle took a sip of sweet nectar, then glanced up at Joy. The little wood satyr had settled herself on a tree trunk and was drinking the sap that seeped from the bark.

"It's *not* a joke," Dazzle said to her friends. "Joy really does drink tree sap."

"I bet it doesn't taste as good as nectar," Twinkle replied as she sipped from a bluebell.

When the butterflies had finished drinking, Joy flew to join them.

"Now I'm going to show you around my beautiful home, Bluebell Wood," Joy announced proudly. "Follow me!" She darted off over the nodding heads of the bluebells.

"Joy has lots of energy, doesn't she?" Twinkle said as the butterflies flew after their new friend.

Joy came to a stop above a patch of rich green leaves.

"This is wild mint," she called. "Come and smell the leaves!"

Dazzle, Twinkle, Skipper, and Mallow fluttered down onto the plant below.

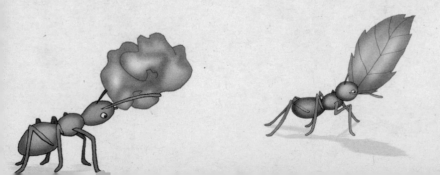

"It smells wonderful," said Dazzle, breathing in the deep, minty scent. Suddenly, a little voice rang through the air. "Good morning, Joy!"

Dazzle peeked over the edge of the leaf. Below, she saw a line of black ants, marching through the bluebells. They carried tiny bits of leaves and twigs.

"Oh, hi!" Joy called back. She fluttered down and hovered near the ant at the front of the line. "What are you doing?"

"We're busy collecting pieces for our anthill," the leader replied. "Let's move!"

Joy waved her wing at the ants as

they marched off. Then she ducked under the thick carpet of mint leaves, out of sight.

"Joy seems to have lots of friends," Dazzle whispered to Skipper as they waited for the little wood satyr to pop out again. But she didn't appear.

"Joy!" Mallow peered into the patch of mint. "Are you OK?"

"Why isn't she coming out?" Dazzle asked.

"I hope she didn't get her wings trapped under there," Twinkle said, looking worried.

"Joy!" Skipper shouted. "Where are you?"

CHAPTER FOUR

Fluffy Friends

Suddenly, Joy popped out of the
clump of leaves, making the other
butterflies jump.

"SURPRISE!" she shouted. "I told
you I like to play jokes, didn't I? Now,
what can I show you next?" She whizzed
off between the trees.

As the rest of them
followed, Joy swooped
lower to the ground.
She hovered near a
hole dug into the side
of a grassy hill.

"Look inside," she told her new friends.

Dazzle, Skipper, Mallow, and Twinkle
peered in. A big red fox was lying asleep
inside, nose on its paws.

"Oh," Dazzle whispered. "I've never
seen a fox this close-up before." Its tail
looked so soft and fluffy!

Joy hovered in front of the hole. "Do
you think I could land on the fox's nose
without waking it?" she asked with a
sly smile.

"No, don't!" Dazzle said quickly.

"The fox might be angry if we wake it up," Twinkle added anxiously.

"All right," Joy agreed. Leaving the fox asleep, she led her new friends farther into the woods. They came to a little winding stream. The crystal-clear water bubbled over pebbles and rocks.

"This is my very favorite place to visit," Joy explained, circling the rocky bank. "I love to sit here in the sun."

"You have a wonderful home, Joy," said Mallow, flying slowly over the cool water.

"There are so many amazing things to see and do," Skipper added.

Joy paused for a moment. "Do you want to see the most *amazing* creature ever?" she said.

"Of course we do!" Dazzle cried.

Immediately, Joy spun around and fluttered off. The other butterflies rushed after her. What could this creature be?

When Dazzle and the others caught up with Joy, she was hovering next to a tree and peeking inside a hole in the trunk.

28

"Oh!" Joy gasped happily. "They've grown even more."

Dazzle peered into the tree hollow, too. She saw two small, feathery creatures sitting side by side in a cozy nest. They had big, round eyes and blinked sleepily as they stared at the five butterflies.

"They're baby owls!" Joy declared.

CHAPTER FIVE

Trouble

"They're so cute," Dazzle whispered.

"Yes, but I think Joy woke them up," Skipper remarked. Dazzle could see the baby owls wriggling in their nest.

Joy danced around the tree hollow. "They're sweet, aren't they? Their mom's not here, but we can still visit."

"Are you sure, Joy?" Mallow asked. "I thought owls slept during the day."

"Oh, it's fine," Joy insisted. "Why don't you say hello to them?"

"Hello," Dazzle called softly. "I'm Dazzle, and these are my friends Twinkle, Mallow, and Skipper."

The baby owls blinked at her with their big eyes.

"I'm Hoot," said one.

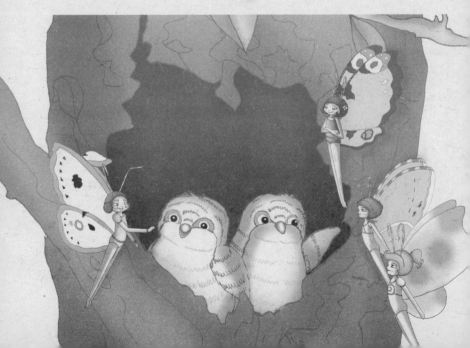

"And I'm Blink," the
other added. "Hi, Joy!
You came back."

"I promised I would,
and I always keep my
promises." Joy smiled. "Will you show
our new friends your special trick?"

Hoot and Blink both swiveled their
heads — all the way around! Dazzle,
Mallow, Skipper, and Twinkle
watched in awe as the baby owls
twisted their heads back to the front
again.

"That's amazing!" Dazzle said.
"Doesn't it hurt?"

Hoot laughed. "No, it's fun!"

"It means we can have eyes in the
backs of our heads," said Blink.

"Oh, *please* do it again," Twinkle begged.

The baby owls swiveled their heads around again, but stopped suddenly. Wide-eyed, they stared past the butterflies.

"What's the matter?" Joy asked.

The baby owls did not reply. They blinked, and Dazzle could see their feathers trembling.

Dazzle turned to see what Hoot and Blink were staring at. A huge owl swooped through the trees — straight toward them. Her dark eyes glared at the butterflies.

"Oh!" Dazzle gasped. "That owl looks angry."

"That's our mom," Hoot said quietly.

The butterflies darted away from the

34

tree as the mother owl
flew closer. Dazzle
could feel the rush of
air from her flapping
wings.

"How are my
babies?" asked the
mother owl as she
landed. She spread
her wings protectively
over Hoot and Blink,
and they cuddled
close to her. "You
should be asleep!"

She turned to look
sternly at Dazzle and
the other butterflies.
Joy had crept to hide
behind them.

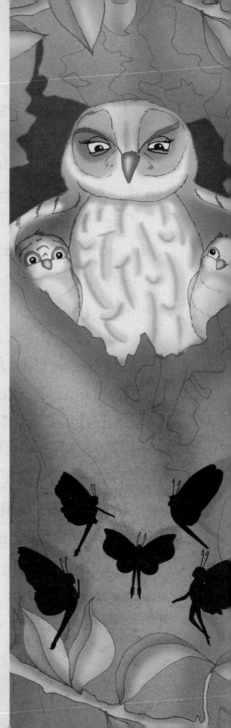

"Please leave right away," the mother owl said. "My babies need to sleep."

"Sorry we disturbed you," Twinkle said politely. "Sweet dreams!"

The mother owl ruffled her feathers and glared at them.

Dazzle felt awful. *We should never have disturbed the baby owls*, she thought. But Joy had told them it would be okay!

The butterflies fluttered away.

"Joy, you shouldn't have woken Hoot and —" Mallow began. But Joy had already zipped off toward a different tree.

"Look," she called. "What's in there?"

"Watch where you're going!" Dazzle cried as Joy tumbled right inside a hole in the tree's trunk.

Dazzle and the others rushed over.

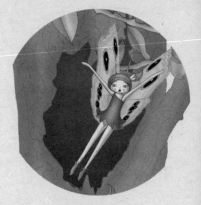

Suddenly, they heard a cry of surprise from inside the tree. A few seconds later, Joy bolted out at top speed.

"Quick!" she shouted. "Fly as fast as you can!"

Dazzle and the others raced off with Joy close behind. Dazzle could hear a dull droning noise swelling in the air behind them.

"Oh, no!" Mallow yelled. "Hornets!"

Dazzle glanced back over her wings as Joy caught up.

A cloud of winged yellow-and-black insects was chasing them!

CHAPTER SIX

The Chase

"Joy, you disturbed a hornets' nest!"
Twinkle cried as the butterflies darted
through the trees. "Hornets are
dangerous when they're angry."

"Stay close to me," Joy yelled,
her wings trembling as she flew. "I
know all the best places to hide in
Bluebell Wood."

Joy made a sharp turn to the right, and the other butterflies followed. They ducked behind a tree. Then Joy swooped down into a patch of tall grass. Dazzle and the others did the same, hiding among the blades of grass.

"The hornets won't see us here," Joy whispered, folding her wings.

Dazzle stayed very still, clinging onto a piece of grass next to Skipper. She hoped Joy was right.

"Where did those butterflies go?"
Dazzle heard a hornet yell as they
buzzed around the tree.

"There they are!" another hornet
shouted. "I can see their colorful wings
in that patch of grass!"

"Let's get out of here!" yelled Joy.

The butterflies zoomed away . . . and
the hornets swarmed after them.

The butterflies dipped and zigzagged
through the woods, trying to lose the

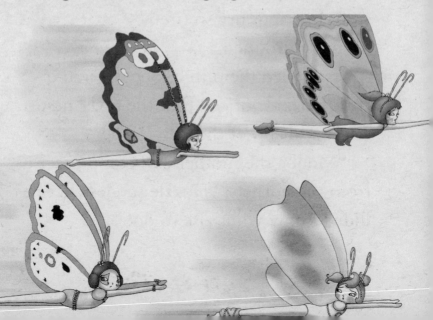

hornets. But when Dazzle glanced back again, it was clear that the hornets weren't giving up. They were gaining on the butterflies! Dazzle could see their yellow-and-black striped bodies and their angry faces.

"We'll *never* outfly the hornets," Skipper shouted as they whizzed over the fox's den. "What are we going to do?"

"My wings are so tired," Twinkle groaned.

As Joy led them in a loop around a tree, Dazzle noticed that the owls' nest was up ahead of them.

"Maybe the mother owl can protect us from the hornets," Dazzle suggested. She didn't know what else to do!

"But that means we'll have to wake them up again," Mallow pointed out.

"This is an emergency!" Twinkle declared. "It's our only hope."

The butterflies dodged through the trees until they reached the owls' nest. Then they all zipped inside the tree.

The owls were asleep. The mother was using her wings to shield the babies. As the butterflies fluttered around them,

the owls opened their eyes and blinked sleepily.

"You again," the mother owl said with a sigh. "I thought I told you we had to sleep?"

"Oh, please, don't be mad," Dazzle pleaded. "A crowd of angry hornets is chasing us, and we need somewhere safe to hide!"

The mother owl swiveled her head and listened. They could all hear a buzzing noise outside the tree — and it was getting louder.

"The hornets are coming for us," Joy whispered.

"Please let them hide here, Mom," said Hoot and Blink together.

The mother owl looked at each of the

butterflies in turn. Then she nodded.
"Get behind me, quickly!" she said.

Shaking with fear, Dazzle and
the others slipped out of sight behind the
mother owl. Now the humming sound
was so loud it filled the tree hollow.
Dazzle was too scared to look!

"Sorry to disturb you, owls," said a
gruff voice. "But have you seen any
pesky butterflies around here?"

CHAPTER SEVEN

Joy's Lesson

Dazzle peeked out from behind the mother owl's wings. She saw an angry hornet hovering in the entrance to the tree hollow. A whole army of hornets was behind him!

Dazzle was about to slip behind the mother owl again when the hornet leader spotted her.

"Got you!" he shouted, pointing his
wing at her.

The mother owl ruffled up her
feathers and gently pushed Dazzle
behind her.

"There are no butterflies here of
interest to you," she said haughtily.
"Now, please leave. My babies need their
sleep."

Dazzle thought the mother owl was
being very kind, but she didn't want to
get the owls into trouble, either. She took
a deep breath and fluttered out. The
other butterflies couldn't believe their eyes!

"She's being very brave," Twinkle
whispered to Mallow.

"We're so sorry," Dazzle said to the
hornet leader, dipping her head. She
looked up at him and tried to smile.

The hornet glared at her. "You
shouldn't go into someone's home
without an invitation," he snapped.
"It's not polite."

"It wasn't Dazzle's fault," said a small
voice. "It was mine." Joy flew out from
behind the mother owl and hovered in
the air next to Dazzle.

"I didn't mean
to," Joy explained to
the hornet. "I just
wasn't watching
where I was going!
I'm sorry."

The hornet
turned to the others
and they buzzed in low voices.

Please forgive us, Dazzle thought. *We'll
never disturb you again!*

"OK," the hornet leader said at last, turning back to Joy and Dazzle. "We accept your apology."

"Thank goodness," Twinkle murmured as the other butterflies crept out, too.

The mother owl looked at Joy. "I hope you've learned an important lesson now, Joy," she said gently. "You must be more careful in the future."

Joy hung her head. "I just wanted my

new friends to like me," she mumbled. "Maybe I *was* showing off a bit."

Dazzle felt sorry for Joy. She didn't like to see their new friend looking so unhappy.

"The rainbow led us to you," she reminded Joy. "That means we'll be special friends forever!"

Joy instantly brightened up.

"As long as we don't disturb any more hornets," Dazzle added with a smile.

CHAPTER EIGHT

Back to the Meadow

"Good-bye," said the hornet leader. The group of hornets flew off, buzzing and calling farewell.

"Thank you," Joy said to the mother owl, and her friends all joined her. Dazzle gave Hoot and Blink butterfly kisses and waved good-bye.

When they had left the owls' nest, Joy
turned to the others. "I have an idea
about how we can really thank the
owls," she whispered. "Follow me."

Dazzle and her friends flew down
from the tree and joined Joy in a patch
of dandelions. Joy fluttered from plant to
plant, sending fuzzy white seeds drifting
into the air.

"We can waft these soft seeds up to

the owls' nest to make it
more comfortable," Joy
explained. "Will you
help me?"

"Of course," Skipper
agreed.

Mallow and Skipper
began shaking the
dandelions, sending the
seeds into the air. Joy,
Dazzle, and Twinkle
wafted them higher
and higher with their
wings toward the tree
hollow. The mother
owl hopped around
with delight when she
realized what they
were doing.

"*Too-hooo!*" she cried happily. She flew out of the tree and helped the butterflies guide the fluffy seeds into the nest.

"Oh, that's so cozy," Hoot said happily, settling down in the nest again.

"Thank you so much," said the mother owl.

"Thank *you*," Dazzle replied. "It was very kind of you to hide us from the hornets."

"We need to go home to Butterfly

Meadow now," Mallow told Dazzle,
Skipper, and Twinkle. "We've been away
for a long time!"

"I'll come with you to the edge of the
woods," said Joy.

The butterflies headed off together,
calling good-bye to their sleepy
owl friends.

"Can't you stay and play a little
longer?" asked Joy when they reached
the edge of the forest. "I'm meeting my
friends at the stream soon. You could
come with me!"

"Thanks for the invitation," Dazzle
said, "but we should go home to
Butterfly Meadow. Our friends might
start to worry about us!"

Joy nodded. "I understand," she said.
"My friends would worry if I was gone

for a long time, too. Good–bye, then,
and have a safe trip home."

"Good–bye!" cried Dazzle, Twinkle,
Skipper, and Mallow as they soared up
into the air.

As they flew, Dazzle glanced back
over her shoulder. Joy was doing her
beautiful bouncing dance as she watched
them go.

"We'll visit Joy again someday,
right?" asked Twinkle.

"Of course we will," Dazzle said.
"When a rainbow leads you to a
butterfly like Joy, you don't forget. We'll
definitely visit her again soon!"

FUN FACTS!
The Super Owl

Have you ever wanted to have superhuman abilities? Fly to school instead of walking? Hear what your teacher whispers in the hall? Cartoon characters aren't the only ones with super skills. Check out the amazing abilities of the owl!

It's hard to hide from an owl. An owl's eyesight is better for things that are far away than up close. Owls can't move their eyes like we can. They can only look straight ahead and have to turn their heads to see what's around them. Some owls can even turn their heads backwards. Imagine being able to see what's behind you without turning your body!

An owl's ears are close to its eyes. Some owls have such good ears that they can locate another animal just by the sound they're making.

Have you ever heard an owl's hoot? Some people think owls are curious because of their hoot, which sounds like a question: "Who?" But owls make lots of sounds, including hooting, whistling, screaming, purring, clicking, and hissing.

Owls also know how to be quiet. Owls' feathers are special. They reduce the sound of air moving around an owl's wing. This means that owls can fly silently and sneak up on other animals.

You can't see an owl's special skills at a glance. What extraordinary talents are *you* hiding?

Dazzle is at home in

Butterfly Meadow!

Here's a sneak peek at her next adventure,

Zippy's Tall Tale

CHAPTER ONE

A New Arrival

"Oh, I can't wait to hear what happened next!" Dazzle gasped. She settled down on a silky red poppy and looked at the glowworms sitting on the grass below her. "Go on, tell us the rest of the story."

Tonight, Dazzle was staying up late with her best friends, Skipper, Mallow,

and Twinkle. The other butterflies in the
meadow had already gone to sleep, but
Dazzle and her friends were perched on
wildflowers in the middle of Butterfly
Meadow. The glowworms had come to
join the fun, too! They were telling the
four butterflies how they'd escaped
from a lizard who was trying to
eat them.

"He chased us all over the field," one
of the glowworms said. "We were so
scared! He kept snapping at us with his
forked tongue."

"Did he catch you?" asked Skipper,
her eyes wide.

"No. We spotted a really thick clump
of grass," another glowworm explained.
"We hid there so that the lizard couldn't
see our glow. Eventually, he went away."

"What a close call!" Dazzle said with a tiny shiver.

"Ooh, my turn!" Twinkle called excitedly. She fluttered around, her red and blue wings shining in the glowworms' light. 'I've got a wonderful story — it's called 'The Day My Wings Looked Especially Beautiful.' "

Dazzle tried not to giggle. Twinkle was a peacock butterfly, and she was *very* proud of the colors on her wings.

"It was a sunny day," Twinkle began. "I was flying through a field not far from here, when I saw something *magical*."

"What?" Dazzle asked breathlessly.

Before Twinkle could go on, she was interrupted by a loud rustling noise. A patch of grass nearby began to sway — but there was no breeze! Just then,

Dazzle spotted a glint of orange among the green. Suddenly, a big orange-and-black butterfly rose up from between the blades of grass. He flew to a flat rock nearby and settled there, batting his magnificent wings slowly back and forth. He glanced at the other butterflies and the glowworms, his eyes twinkling.

"Hello!" Mallow called. "Welcome to Butterfly Meadow."

"Hello to you, too!" the butterfly called back. Dazzle could see that there were black bands speckled with white spots around the edges of his orange wings. "My name's Zippy, and I'm a monarch butterfly. I'm migrating south." He heaved a sigh. "But it's such a long way! I've flown hundreds of miles, and I haven't spoken to any other butterflies for *ages*."

"I'm Dazzle, and these are my friends, Skipper, Mallow, Twinkle, and the glowworms," Dazzle explained. "Would you like to join us?"

Zippy cleared his throat, looking happy. "Well, I *was* listening to those stories you were telling," he said eagerly. "I have the most exciting story to share with you. It's about the time I wrestled a bear."

Dazzle couldn't wait to hear Zippy's story!

SPECIAL EDITION

More Rainbow Magic Fun!
Three Stories in One!

SCHOLASTIC
www.scholastic.com
www.rainbowmagiconline.com

HiT entertainment

SPFAIRIES

RAINBOW magic™

There's Magic in Every Series!

The Rainbow Fairies

The Weather Fairies

The Jewel Fairies

The Pet Fairies

The Fun Day Fairies

The Petal Fairies

The Dance Fairies

Read them all!

www.scholastic.com

www.rainbowmagiconline.com

RMFAIRY